Happy Birthday
Gianna
Kelly + Mister Spunky

S0-DVF-262

Mister Spunky and His Friends

(Based, roughly, on a true story.)

Kelly Preston

Copyright © 2013 Kelly Preston

All rights reserved.

ISBN: 1484966570
ISBN-13: 978-1484966570

DEDICATION

I would like to take this time to give praise and thanks to God. God has blessed me with four beautiful dogs with special needs and a wonderful family and friends. I also would like to give a dedication to those with special needs (pets and humans); thank you for teaching all of us how to be a better person, love each other and help each other with no expectations.

A special dedication goes out to Corridor Therapy Dogs, for all the work you do in schools, libraries, hospitals, care centers, and other facilities needing therapy animals. Enriching young students with learning challenges overcome those obstacles with therapy dogs right by these children's sides. Thank you for your dedicated work.

We are delighted to be in partnership with Corridor Therapy Dogs, assisting children and adults with reading and other learning challenges.

Kelly

ACKNOWLEDGMENTS

Editor In Chief: Jerry Payne
www.yourcopywriter.net

Illustrations and Cover Design: Magical Creations Studio
www.magicalcreationsstudio.com

Photography: Heather Martin
www.photographybyheathermartin.zenfolio.com

Corridor Therapy Dogs
Dedicated to enriching the lives of others
www.corridortherapydogs.com

Mister Spunky was the happiest dog in the world (and the coolest!). He loved driving around in his red convertible, with the top down, and his sunglasses on.

Mister Spunky was carefree and happy-go-lucky. He enjoyed life and loved to have fun.

One day, Mister Spunky was on his way to the beach. He loved the beach. He loved the sunshine and the sand and he loved to play in the waves. He even brought his surfboard along. And there was an ice cream stand at the beach with special ice cream and frozen treats that were just for dogs.

As he was driving along the freeway to the beach, Mister Spunky noticed a small, frightened dog on the side of the road. At first, Mister Spunky kept going. He didn't want to stop. He wanted to get to the beach.

But Mister Spunky couldn't stop thinking about the frightened, little dog, so he turned around and went back. "What's the matter, little dog?" he asked. But the little dog said nothing and hid behind a tree. The little dog had been bullied by other dogs and was afraid Mister Spunky would bully her, too.

But Mister Spunky said, "Don't be afraid, little dog. I can be your friend. I can make sure that nothing hurts you. There's nothing to be afraid of if you have a friend around. Come with me in my cool convertible! We're going to the beach where we can play in the waves!"

The frightened little dog thought about it for a long time and then decided to be friends with Mister Spunky. "Woof!" she said, and Mister Spunky answered, "Woof!" and the two drove off for the beach together and the frightened little dog, who said her name was Buffy, wasn't frightened anymore.

Soon, Mister Spunky and Buffy passed a dog on the side of the road who was growling and barking. Mister Spunky kept driving. He wanted to get to the beach! But then he decided to turn around and see why the dog was so angry.

"What's the matter?" said Buffy to the angry dog but the angry dog said nothing and just kept growling.

"Don't be mad," said Buffy "You probably just feel unloved. But Mister Spunky and I can be your friends. There's nothing to be mad at if you have friends around. Come along with us! We're going to the beach!"

The angry dog thought about it for a long time and then decided to be friends with Buffy and Mister Spunky. "Woof!" she said, and Mister Spunky and Buffy both answered, "Woof!" Then the three drove off for the beach together and the angry dog, who said her name was Carla, didn't feel unloved anymore and was no longer angry.

Soon, Mister Spunky, Buffy, and Carla passed a very tiny dog on the side of the road who couldn't walk. They pulled over and Carla asked the very tiny dog, "What's the matter, tiny dog? Why can't you walk?"

The tiny dog answered that she could walk, but she couldn't see where she was going. "I am blind," said the very tiny dog, "and so I am afraid to move."

"Come along with us," said Carla. "We'll be your friends and we'll take care of you! You never have to worry when you're with friends who love and take care of each other. We're going to the beach!"

The tiny dog thought about it for a long time and then decided to be friends with Mister Spunky, Buffy, and Carla. "Woof!" said the very tiny dog who said her name was Miss Sunshine. "Woof!" said Mister Spunky, Buffy, and Carla.

Then the four dogs all drove off for the beach together where they played in the waves and had frozen dog treats. Now they are all friends and they are all happy. And they have fun and exciting adventures wherever they go!

And Mister Spunky, who was the happiest dog in the world, is even happier!

– End –

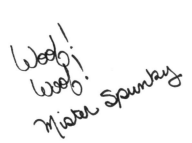

ABOUT THE AUTHOR

Kelly Preston, award winning author of **Real Dogs Don't Whisper** (www.realdogsdontwhisper.com), is first and foremost, an animal lover. Raised on a ten-acre property in a small town in Pennsylvania, she grew up with horses, rabbits, and dogs.

When she left home after college, she acquired Gizmo, an irresistible Lhasa Apso that started her on a journey full of joys and sorrows, hopes and tribulations, frustrations, endless lessons in patience, and above all else, love. All of this has come at the hands (more precisely the paws) of Gizmo, Betty Boop, Buffy, Carla Mae, and the inimitable Mr. MaGoo.

Real Dogs Don't Whisper: Life Lessons from a Larger than Life Dog is the story of Kelly Preston and her experiences with her special needs dogs and how they have learned, grown and thrived together. *Real Dogs Don't Whisper* is more than a book about dogs, it's a book about life.

Buffy

Betty Boop (Miss Sunshine)

Carla Mae

Mr MaGoo (Mister Spunky)

Coloring
Activities

19925548R00022

Made in the USA
Charleston, SC
18 June 2013